Also by Bob Garvey:
Holy Spirit Tours, Winter Excursion daily meditations
A Catholic Moment, weblog of daily readings and reflections:
   https://www.acatholic.org/author/bobgarvey/

More books from Home Crafted Artistry & Printing
A Heart for Truth by Joyce Cordell
His Beauty Unveiled by Anita K Bube
Echo Beach by Nancy Parson
One Step Closer by Geri Manning
Lines Fallen in Pleasant Places by Louise Louis Hill
Five Generations, Stories from My Father by Ron Aubrey
Sunday Mass, What's It All About? by Robert W Bibb
A Journey of Thought, Seven Booklets by Robert W Bibb
Across the Generations compiled by Carol Chandler-Russ
Fantastic Snowflakes by Mary Bibb Smith
Wrong Side of the Tracks, Right Side of Life by Daniel Easter
Stand Straight and Grow Tall by Dolores Howell
Nature's Four Season by Julie Whittenberg
To God with Love by Julie Whittenberg
Miraculous Interventions *series* - Deborah Aubrey-Peyron
   Now includes eight books plus two "Best Of" issues
ALSO by Deborah Aubrey-Peyron:
   Let's Take a Walk, Dave The Story of Dave Becker
   Christmas Chaos!
   Deb's Christmas Cookbook, a Collection of Recipes
   An Old Man's Christmas - - with Ron Aubrey
Albert's Song by Dr Rev Stephen E Ellis
Animals in Heaven by Dr Rev Stephen E Ellis
Darkest Knight by Dr Rev Stephen E Ellis
Hell Is Waiting by Dr Rev Stephen E Ellis
Is There Really a God? by Dr Rev Stephen E Ellis
50 Questions for God by Dr Rev Stephen E Ellis
Look for all these and more at:
   HomeCraftedArtistry.com
   Also available at Amazon.com

What about God?

A discussion of eternal proportions

Bob Garvey

Home Crafted Artistry & Printing
Lanesville, Indiana

ISBN: 978-1-7360304-3-1

Home Crafted Artistry & Printing
2404 Scenic Drive NE, #6
Lanesville, IN 47136
HomeCraftedArtistry@yahoo.com

You can contact Bob at: bgarvey@aol.com

What about God?

Chapter 1

"Why do you go to Church on Sunday, do you still believe in that God stuff?" Parker challenged his friend Matt.

"Yes," Matt answered in a defensive tone.

"Have you ever seen God, heard him or smelled him? How can you believe in something that you can't even see? That God stuff is made up," Parker continued.

"Yeh, but the Bible states clearly that there is a God and that he is real," retorted Matt.

"The Bible? You've gotta be kidding. That stuff is a bunch of made-up stuff that religious people wrote to make money. You went to St. Z's didn't you? Don't you remember when they said that the Bible is just a collection of religious fairy tales? Grow up Matt, quit falling for the religion stuff."

"They didn't say it was fairy tales. I really can't remember what they said about it, but, I admit, they didn't seem to think the Bible was all that important," Matt answered.

"Okay," Parker went on, "God is a made-up idea to keep you in line, and the Bible has nothing to do with real life, so why do you go to Church? I know why. Because your mom makes you go, right?"

"Well, not exactly. Yeh, my mom makes me go but I guess I could stay home if I put up a fight," replied Matt.

"Look. Your parents are from the old generation that didn't have the education we have. They weren't allowed to think for themselves. They went along with religion because everyone else did. Can they prove that God exists? Can they prove that whatever is in the Bible is true? Of course not. Next year, when you leave home and go to college, you can leave that Church stuff behind and make a life for yourself," Parker concluded.

"Well, I have to admit that when I ask mom why I have to go to Church, she says, 'Because I said so. As long as you're living under this roof you go to Church!' She has never explained to me why she goes to Church, except that she wants to go to heaven when she dies. Don't say it Parker. I know you're going to try to make me prove that there really is a place called 'heaven.' I can't answer that one either. So, before we start hating each other, let's change the subject," Matt conceded.

Matt left the conversation confused and upset, so he decided to talk to Fr. Tom, the school chaplain and see if he had answers to Parker's challenging questions.

Matt shared with Fr. Tom the gist of his conversation with his friend. Is there a God? How do we know? Is there a heaven? Can it be proved? Is the Bible true or not?

Fr. Tom began by asking Matt, "Prove to me that trees exist, Matt."

Matt: "Well, look out the window there's a bunch of them."

Fr. Tom: "I can't see that far, why should I take your word for it?"

Matt: "Come outside with me and I'll let you touch one."

Fr. Tom: "Not me, I like the air-conditioned room we're in. How do I know you aren't lying to me? Besides define "tree" for me.

Matt: "Okay, I give up. If you are so closed to my suggestions, it's impossible for me to convince you that trees exist."

Fr. Tom: "Same with God. If someone is dead set against believing in the possibility of God, then no matter what you say, you will not convince them. Can't make headway with a closed mind."

Fr. Tom: "Now let's assume Parker has an open mind and is truly searching for the truth, then we might get through to him."

Fr. Tom: "First of all if you can't see, hear, or touch something does that mean it doesn't exist? Are there things that exist which we can't see?

Matt: "The wind I guess. You can't see it but it exists. And electricity is invisible but it can kill you if you aren't careful...you can't see electricity."

Fr. Tom: "Good thinking Matt. What about love. What does it smell like? What's its color? It exists doesn't it? Why does your mom work so hard to pay your way through school, cook meals for you, clean your clothes? Is it because she is a robot that's been programmed to do this stuff? No, it's because she loves you. And the love in her heart can't be weighed, seen, or smelled, can it."

Matt: "Yeh, and what about cell phone waves. They are crisscrossing like crazy across this room right now, and we can't stick out our hands and catch them or stop them. They exist and they are invisible."

Fr. Tom: "We could probably think of many more examples. Point is, Matt that many things exist that cannot be seen. So, saying that God can't be seen proves nothing. Agreed?"

Matt: "Hmm. I wish I had thought to say that to Parker."

Fr. Tom: "On the other hand, Parker has a point. Ideas cannot be seen, but they still exist, and they have great power. Someone had the idea of inventing an airplane. And when he followed up on it, look what happened. Communists are people who bought into the ideas of a man named Karl Marx. They claim that the world will live happily ever after if his ideas are put into practice. The fact is, where communism has been tried, people live "miserably ever after." And there are TV products that claim to work miracles but don't. Ideas can be dangerous. You have to be skeptical and discerning about what people try to sell you. So back to God. Is God a hoax or real? The fact that we can't see him doesn't prove a thing."

Fr. Tom: "How do you know the wind exists? It makes leaves move and trees bend. How do you know radio waves exist? You can get music on your cell phone. These invisible realities can't be seen, but their effects can. What does God do that proves to us he's real?"

Matt: "Well I remember when Tony went on the youth retreat. Something happened there. He said he met Jesus and that Jesus changed his life. Tony doesn't do pot any more or hang around with loose girls. Even though he didn't see Jesus, something happened that changed his life."

Fr. Tom: "Great example. Jesus is so real and so powerful that he was able to change a kid like Tony during the course of a weekend retreat. Have you had such an experience of the "invisible" Jesus?"

Matt: "No. I passed on the youth retreat. I didn't want to give up a whole weekend to be stuck in a place where people talked about religion all day. Maybe I should have given it a try."

Fr. Tom: "You don't have to go on a youth retreat to prove Jesus exists. And, if at Sunday Mass, all you do is gawk around the Church and look at the girls, you probably won't find Jesus there either. If you were able to meet Jesus and he changed your life, then you'd have proof, just like Tony, that Jesus exists."

Fr. Tom: "Another question. Prove to me that money exists."

Matt: "Oh no, here we go again. Here's a dollar bill. You can see it and touch it, so it exists. You can even buy something with it. Does that prove it to you?"

Fr. Tom: "You win this time, Matt. However, there are many people who don't really care whether money exists or not. Take little kids before they are old enough to spend money. They see coins and bills, but it's just stuff to them—like markers on a game board. It isn't real until they want to buy something and need money to get it. Then money begins to really exist for them. Same with God. If someone doesn't see a need for God, they can't get too excited about whether or not he exists, can they?"

Fr. Tom: "Let's go back to Tony. I knew Tony was going through a tough time at home, and that he was getting led down the wrong road in his social life. I went out of my way to befriend him and challenged him to try the retreat. I told him that after the first night, if he wanted to go back home, I would take him. Tony consented, reluctantly. The first night he heard another kid, just like him, talk about how Jesus changed his life. Tony was hooked. He wanted what the other kid had, so he stayed willingly for the weekend."

Fr. Tom: "With you Matt, you have chosen good friends. You have a stable home life, and you get good grades in school. Things are working out pretty well for you, so why would you need God? Why would you need Jesus? This is like a useless idea to you; the way money is to a three-year old."

Matt: "Fr. Tom you see the outside of me, but you don't see the inside. Even though I have friends to hang out with, deep inside I'm lonely. I can't really talk about what bothers me with my parents. And, what hurts most, is that the only girl friend I ever had, got tired of me and chose a better-looking, richer kid. When I think about that, something deep inside really hurts."

Fr. Tom: "That's called rejection, Matt. All of us have felt it in one way or another. I am honored that you trust me enough to tell me what's going on inside you. You don't have Tony's problems, but you do have something that qualifies you to look for Jesus. Take my word on what I am about to say. Everyone has an aching inside them. Everyone deals in some way with loneliness. When I was a teenager, I kept up a front to make me feel accepted by my peers. I tried to avoid my parents because they kept asking me questions. And I had some dates, but nothing too serious. Though things looked good on the outside of my life, I felt an emptiness inside. Though I didn't realize it, I was looking for Jesus. My cousin Jason invited me to a prayer meeting that he went to. It was kind of crazy with people singing, raising their hands, and reading the Bible. At first, I wanted to run away. Then I kind of liked the way I felt when the meeting was over, so I kept going. One night, the leader of the meeting asked if anyone wanted to accept Jesus as their savior, Lord, and best friend. I'm surprised I had the courage to raise my hand, but I did. Jesus came into my heart that night and that inner emptiness I felt was gone forever. Down the road, I felt a call from God to be a priest and dedicate my life to bringing Jesus to others, especially young people."

Matt: "Wow. I wish I could go to that kind of prayer meeting."

Fr. Tom: "I'm not sure those kinds of meetings exist in this area, but I'll give you another suggestion. We have Eucharistic adoration on Friday nights. Even if you aren't sure about the existence of God or if Jesus is real, just sit there looking at the monstrance. Relax and pretend that Jesus is there. Talk to him. Ask him your questions. Tell him how you feel. Ask him to show you he's real. And, if you want to, you can even ask him to come into your heart and remove some of the pain of rejection you've been feeling."

Fr. Tom: "Try it one time, then come back, and let's talk about your experience. We want proof that Jesus is real to you. See if something of what happened to Tony begins to happen in you in a more gradual way."

Matt: "Okay, Fr. Tom, I will give it a try. And if nothing happens, I will be totally honest with you about it. I don't want to hurt your feelings, but I will tell the truth. I still have some "Parker "in me and am skeptical about God being real. Thanks for taking time with me today. Can we talk about the Bible sometime?"

Fr. Tom: "Sure. That's what I'm here for."

Chapter 2

Matt: "Okay, Fr. Tom. I did feel more peaceful after going to adoration. There is something real about the host. It, of course, is real. But I kind of felt some rays of something coming out from it and landing on me. Nothing spectacular but it definitely affected me. That feeling of rejection has begun to go away too. I will keep trying the adoration and keep you informed as to how it works out."

Matt: "Now what about the Bible? Is it just a bunch of made up stories?"

Fr. Tom: "Who told you that it is a bunch of made-up stories? Aren't all stories made up? That doesn't mean they aren't true."

Matt: "Well the religion teachers say that they are just made up. We don't have to take it too seriously. Like, Adam and Eve didn't really exist. It was all made up."

Fr. Tom: "I am not out to defend your religion teachers, but something tells me that you are giving an over-simplified version of their classes. Some stories in the Bible are "made up" and others are factual. Just as some novels are fiction and others are non-fiction. A lot of kids take from religion classes what they want to hear. If teachers do not take the Bible seriously, they are not allowed to teach in the school. I think you know that."

Fr. Tom: "Okay, let's start with a made-up story. What about, "The Three Little Pigs?" Were there really three pigs who tried to build houses for themselves? Was there really a big bad wolf who ate them, and slid down the chimney? But is there truth in the story?"

Matt: "Well I guess there is truth. The story writer is telling us to be careful about how we build our lives, and that there are forces out in the world that want to destroy us. I guess the pig who used brick is the model to follow rather than his careless brothers who took the easy way-out using straw and sticks. And I've been around enough to know that there are people who are trying to take advantage of kids and leading them into dangerous places—like drug-dealers for example. And in the end the wise pig wins out over the forces of evil. So, "The Three Little Pigs" has important lessons to be learned about life. Even though the story is fictional, it conveys important truth."

Fr. Tom: "Now it's my turn to say 'wow!' I've never heard anyone who has a deeper interpretation of this fairy tale. It would be fun to go through other fairy tales and sift out the lessons they are trying to teach us. Yes, they are entertaining. If they were not, kids wouldn't listen to them. Underneath, however, there are truths to be taught."

Fr. Tom: "You know there are 73 books in the Bible. Some are fiction and some are non-fictional. All of them were written to convey truth—deep truths about God, human nature, and finding the answers to life. The challenge is to dig into each of the books and discover the truth that is being taught. Ask, what did the writer have in mind?

Now, it is the teaching of the Church that these particular books were selected from many others out there, because it is the belief of the Church that these were inspired by the Holy Spirit. This opens up new questions like: Who is the Holy Spirit? How can he write a book? How do we know the Church is authorized to decide which books belong in the Bible and which don't? How come, "The Three Little Pigs" is not a book of the Bible? So, let's just say for now that the Bible teaches truth whether the particular book is meant to be nonfictional or not."

Matt: "What about Adam and Eve. The religion teacher says that they didn't really exist or at least that their names weren't 'Adam' and 'Eve.' Is there any truth hidden in that story?

Fr. Tom: "There are books and books written about this. Did the entire human race come from one man and one woman? It would seem that way, but I don't think that's what the author was trying to teach. (We note that the Church does teach this). Was there really a good tree and a bad tree? Was it an apple tree? Did a snake really talk? Did Adam and Eve sew fig leaves together as clothes? Was there really a gate leading into paradise? Was there a paradise? Lots of questions. What counts, though is the truth that is taught in the story. Can you think of what truth the author was trying to get across?"

Matt: "Well, I guess that as long as Adam and Eve obeyed, they were happy. When the snake came along—the devil? —and tricked them into going against God's rule, they fell for it. When they listened to the devil, they pulled away from God and their lives became miserable. The devil won and God lost. After that Adam and Eve didn't feel like they could trust God anymore, so they hid and tried to avoid him. They bought into the devil's story.... Hmm, the devil made up a story too, didn't he? And his was a lie. He was a slick salesperson who got Adam and Eve to buy a fake product."

Fr. Tom: "Good thinking, Matt. Does the Adam and Eve story have any truth that is relevant to us today?"

Matt: "Well I know temptation is real. And I know I feel better inside when I try to please God. When I do something wrong, I feel guilty and lose a sense of inner peace. Whether or not the devil is real, there is something out there trying to get me to turn away from God. And when I listen to this "something," it usually steals some of my happiness and I don't want to go to Church."

Fr. Tom: "Right on. Like Adam and Eve, life is a struggle for us all. The devil is real, and the Church has lots to teach us about him. There is something unseen inside each of us that knows what brings us closer to God and what pushes us away. We have a "sin detector" built into us. I bet you know the name for this, don't you?"

Matt: "Are you talking about conscience?"

Fr. Tom: "Right again. Our life on this earth is a testing time. We are faced with decisions whether to line up with God or travel the devil's path. In the end if we go God's way, happiness awaits us. If we go with the devil's suggestions, misery awaits us—for eternity. So, this story is fundamental, isn't it? Our whole life is told in that opening story of the Bible. The drama of Adam and Eve is our own drama. The effects of sin on them are also on us.

Getting back into a good relationship with God was the next challenge for Adam and Eve. The same challenge is ours. We wonder whether or not these first people ever got their acts together again, repented, and ended up on good terms with God. No clear answer is given, is it? The rest of the Bible is about God's plan to call man back to himself. Every book of the Bible, in some way, tells our own story—our own journey toward God—and whether or not we ultimately win or lose."

Matt: "So the Bible has fiction and non-fiction. It is inspired by the Holy Spirit. Every book contains truth that connects with us today—how we live our lives and make our choices. But how come so many people find it boring? And how come no one pays attention when it is read at Mass?"

Fr. Tom: "You are putting me on the spot. Some people, incidentally, do pay attention to readings during Mass. Sad to say, it is only a few. Was our discussion of Adam and Eve boring? Why not?

Because we got into the story and tried to apply it to our lives. This is called Bible study."

Matt: "Why don't religion teachers do this--do Bible studies?"

Fr. Tom: "Religion teachers have a nearly impossible task working with teenagers who are not even vaguely interested in the subject. Can you imagine the challenge of holding the interest of high schoolers? Bible studies work best with people who really want to learn and grow, not with kids who are forced to be in a classroom when they'd rather be outside goofing off. You will find that the Bible studies in your Church are much like the kinds of discussions you and I have been having. It is best to read the Bible together with someone else and discuss its meaning. When people start getting deeper into the Bible, they tend to pay closer attention on Sunday to the Scripture readings and to the priests' homilies. Let's face it, many adults in Church are like teenagers. They are there because they have to be, and don't pay much attention to what is read from the Bible. We priests have a challenge on our hands."

Matt: "Okay, Fr. Tom, so maybe I've got the wrong idea about the Bible. So if God exists, if Jesus is real, if the Bible was inspired by the Holy Spirit, and if the Bible helps me get better hold on life, then I guess my next question is how to work Bible reading into my life...or maybe find a Bible study group that I can be part of.

And, by the way, what is the connection of the real Jesus that I see in Church on Friday with reading the Bible?"

Fr. Tom: "You are really putting me to the test, Matt. These are great questions. The fact is, if we are open to it, we meet Jesus every time we read the Bible seriously. How can that happen? Well, it's all about the Holy Spirit, the fact that Jesus is risen and still among us, and that God is working to get each one of us back into a good relationship with him, because he loves us. If you keep asking these great questions, you and I will end up writing a book."

Matt: Thank you for your time Fr. Tom. And oh, by the way, I shared with Parker the idea that there are many things that are real, and you can't see them. He didn't have a comeback for me, but he still doesn't buy into the existence of God. Our discussions are getting deeper, and this time I'm doing most of the talking."

Chapter 3

Matt: "Okay Fr. Tom what about heaven and hell. Do they really exist? My friends think that if there really is a heaven, everyone goes there when they die, even the so-called "bad" people. Do we have proof for the existence of heaven and hell, or do we have to wait till it's all over and find out the hard way?"

Fr. Tom: "Let's go back to Eucharistic adoration. You've found out that Jesus must be real because of the way he impacts you there. Though he is "hidden" within a disguise of a piece of altar bread, he's really there. And Jesus, we Catholics believe, is God also. He is God's Son. He was sent to earth as a man in order to win us over and show us the way back to God. During his stay on earth, he did "hand-to-hand" combat with the devil, and, unlike Adam and Eve, he won the match. His final moment of victory was his death on the cross where Satan was soundly defeated, and his rising from the dead, where he proved he not only has victory over Satan, but victory over death.

All this is a lead in to the fact that since Jesus is God, he speaks the truth. When the writers of the Gospels in the New Testament tell us what Jesus said, they are conveying to us the truth of God. So, to prove something, the first thing we do is to search the words of Jesus to listen to what he has to say.

Jesus is the only person who is in position to tell what goes on outside this world. He came from heaven and returned to heaven, and he told his disciples that he was going to prepare a place for them in heaven too. He also spoke frequently about hell—the consequence for those who decide to cut themselves off from God forever. So, for right now let's use the Gospels to find out what Jesus said on a particular topic. Even atheists accept the fact that Jesus existed, that he was an unusually wise and powerful person, and that his words should be taken seriously—whether or not he was God's Son. I will challenge you, Matt, to read through the Gospel of Matthew, your patron saint, and see how many references are given to life after death—the place of reward and the place of punishment."

Matt: "Okay you're beginning to lose me Fr. Tom. Can you put this in simpler terms?"

Fr. Tom: "I will paraphrase what Jesus said. Read Matthew 7:13. A group of people are walking downtown (this is fiction by the way), it is after dark, and they come to a junction. There are two doors they must choose between. One is wide and there is a lot of noise on the other side—like 4th Street Live. Most all the people are going through that door to be "where the action is." The other door is a narrow one that opens to a street that is rather quiet. Only a few people are going through the narrow door. Every person has to decide on the wide or the narrow door. Jesus comes along and tells us to hop in his helicopter. As we rise into the air, we see what's happening on the other side of the doors. Though the people don't realize it, at the end of the "wide-door street" there is a violent gang. They grab people, beat them up, and toss them into a dump truck. People are screaming and yelling as they are attacked. At the end of the "narrow-door street" there is a big limousine waiting. The few people who travel that street are welcomed into the limousine and taken to a beautiful seaside resort. Jesus returns to the ground and then gives us a choice. Which door would you choose?

Matt: "The narrow one of course, because I realize where it leads."

Fr. Tom: "But most everyone else is going through the wide gate, and probably making fun of you for going the narrow door. Don't you feel tempted to go through the wide door and be like everyone else?"

Matt: "Sure Fr. Tom, but when I realize there is a gang at the end waiting to beat me up, I ignore the comments of the crowd. In fact, I begin to shout out something like "There is destruction waiting for you if you go through that gate. Jesus showed me what's at the end. Change your mind and join me." Even though the wide gate might bring some instant fun, I am thinking of the long run. A few minutes travelling the narrow road is worth it. But what does that have to do with heaven and hell?"

Fr. Tom: "Read Jesus' words. In the Bible he takes us for a "helicopter" ride to show results of our choices. Knowing the end results, we have wisdom to make the right choice."

Matt: "So heaven is the limousine and hell is the gang. Is that it?"

Fr. Tom: "Jesus tells us the truth because he wants us to be happy. Parker will remind you that this "parable" was a made-up story by Jesus. What he won't tell you, however, is that this story conveys perhaps the most important truth there is. And yet, when we look at the world, most people are going happily through the wide gate and travelling toward destruction. They have deafened their ears to Jesus and to the warnings given them by his followers."

Matt: "So each day I am making decisions as to whether to walk through the wide gate or the narrow one. Is it true that Jesus says only "a few" are going through the narrow gate? Is it true that Jesus said the majority of people are heading down the broad road that leads to destruction?"

Fr. Tom: "Read it yourself and see. The world doesn't want to buy into the truth because it wants to live the easy way and still get to heaven. You know life doesn't work this way. Kids who goof off in school don't end up with high grades, do they? There are consequences to our choices. Sadly, our own experience tells us that most people are not taking God seriously or trying to follow the way of Jesus. They don't take time to think about what's at the end of the road they are travelling. Doesn't our own experience convince us that only "a few" are on the right road?"

Matt: "When I think about the guys in my high school classes, it scares me. They think God is a joke, that the Bible is an outdated book, and things will work out fine for them no matter what choices they make in life. Do you think most of these guys are headed towards hell?"

Fr. Tom: "My job is to try to persuade as many as I can to choose the narrow gate. I don't know how peoples' lives will end up. I just try my best to get them to meet Jesus now and to follow him the way you and Tony are doing. It is difficult to get through the narrow gate especially when the popular way is the wide gate, but it is worth the effort. My job as a priest is to do what you were talking about earlier: stand at the juncture of the gates and tell people to come to Jesus and heed his warning. Some will listen and some won't. The price of being popular is not worth the meager results it brings, is it?"

Matt: "Okay, I'll go through Matthew's gospel and try to catch all the times when Jesus talked about the ultimate consequences of our choices in life. I am glad that I've begun doing adoration, because the closer I feel to Jesus, the more I want to be with him forever. And I'm beginning to see that heaven is an expanded version of what happens in my heart on Friday nights. I can't handle the thought that I'd go through eternity without ever being with Jesus again. Meantime, I will start thinking of a question that might stump you. I wish I had begun talking with you when I started high school."

Fr. Tom: "You weren't ready then, I don't think. You needed some experience under your belt.

Meantime, keep delving into the Bible and trying to dig out the hidden truth that's there. The gospels are a good place to start. As you read, more questions will come to your mind. Sit with the questions. Bring them to Jesus on Friday night and notice what he shows you."

Chapter 4

Matt: "Okay, I've got a non-Bible question for you. It came in social studies class. Should we support women's rights or should be opposed to abortion? Abortion is killing little kids, but banning it takes away God-given rights from women. I know what the Church teaches, but the Church is "pro rights" too isn't it? How do you deal with this one Fr. Tom?"

Fr. Tom: "Have you ever heard of Picasso?"

Matt: "Yeh, I think he was a famous artist. That's all I know."

Fr. Tom: "Do you know that his paintings are worth millions of dollars? Now suppose that Picasso rents out a couple of rooms in an apartment complex to do some of his painting. And suppose the owner of the complex decides to go into Picasso's studio and take a few of his paintings and sell them, or worse, destroy them. Do you think Picasso has a right to sue him?"

Matt: "Of course. The owner was guilty of a serious crime."

Fr. Tom: "Was he really? After all he owned the apartment. Doesn't that mean he owns everything in the apartments including Picasso's million-dollar paintings?"

Matt: "I don't know about the law, but the paintings belong to Picasso, not the apartment guy. He has no right to take paintings that belong to someone else. But aren't we getting off track?"

Fr. Tom: "No we're not. Who creates the preborn babies that live inside the bodies of women? Isn't it God? If you read Psalm 139 in the Bible, the writer says that God, "knit him together in his mother's womb." So, who owns the baby? The mother or God? The one who created the baby "owns" it just as Picasso "owns" the masterpieces that he painted. God honors a woman by "housing" his work inside her body. The woman has no more rights over God's creation than the apartment owner has over Picasso's paintings. Do women have the right to take God's works and destroy them? The rights involved here are really God's rights, aren't they? A woman does not have the right to destroy one of God's masterpieces any more than your parents have the right to destroy you."

Matt: "I guess I never thought of God's rights before. Does God really create each new baby that comes into the world? I thought it was the parents who did this."

Fr. Tom: "Of course the parents are involved, but it is God who breathes spirit and life into all of us. If you check out your Bible, one creation story says that God is like a potter. He took clay from the ground, breathed life into it, and Adam came into existence. Of course, this is an analogy. God forms us as a potter forms a work of pottery. Adam and Eve did not just magically appear like a tooth fairy. God had his hand in creating them. And the Bible says he made them in his own "image and likeness." Human beings, in some way, resemble God, just the way you, in some way, resemble your dad and mom."

Matt: "Does that mean I was created by God as well? There was more than my parents involved?"

Fr. Tom: "Yes. In one of his letters St. Paul said that our bodies are not our own. They belong to God. He even said that when we are baptized our bodies become temples of the Holy Spirit! That is why the Church is so insistent in teaching that we must take good care of our bodies. They are God's property, not ours. We have no right to abuse God's masterpieces by misusing drugs, by beating on ourselves, or by using our bodies in illicit sexual behavior. You did not make yourself, Matt. Nor did your parents create you. God had the idea of you in his mind even before your parents met each other, just as an artist has an idea for a painting even before he applies his brush to the canvas. If people deny the existence of God, they must come up with another explanation of how human beings came upon the earth. And if they deny God, they deny that he has any rights."

Matt: "If what you're saying is true, then everything belongs to God since he created it all. Things didn't just happen to "pop up" on the earth. A seed didn't just magically fall into the ground and grow up to be Adam. This blows my mind to think that I belong to God because he is the Artist who put me together. Why didn't they explain this to us in religion class?"

Fr. Tom: "Good question. Maybe you'll be a religion teacher someday and can explain the truth of the Bible to teenagers. Imagine how the world would change if everyone realized they were a creation of God? Imagine how boys would be more respectful to girls if they realized the girls belonged to God. If you want to learn more about this, try looking up "Theology of the Body" and read what Pope John Paul II said about all of this."

Matt: "Okay, Fr. Tom, you've really got me thinking now. By the way I told Parker the story of the two gates. I also dared him to go to Eucharistic adoration with me. I told him that if he really wanted to find out if Jesus is real, go with me on Friday and spend some time there."

Chapter 5

Matt: "Let's talk about going to Church today. Most of the guys I know wouldn't be caught dead in Church. They said that after confirmation, they "graduated" from religion and now have better ways to spend their Sunday mornings. Besides when they went to Church, they got nothing out of it anyway. And they observe that only hypocrites and old ladies go to Church. In a way I agree with them. Most of the time I go to Church I get nothing out of it. I feel like I'm putting in my time because my mom and dad insist that I go. They remind me that I am setting an example for my little brother and sisters."

Fr. Tom: "Let's talk about swimming. You've been on the swim team since freshman year, haven't you Matt? Tell me about practice. How often you go to practice, what time, and what you do."

Matt: "Well we have to be at the pool at six o'clock in the morning Monday through Friday for an hour and a half of practice. The coach really put us through our paces. We have to do calisthenics, weightlifting, and laps. It is tough, but it is worth it. I really got in good shape, and as you know we won the regionals two years in a row."

Fr. Tom: "What if you told the coach that you needed your sleep and would come to practice only when you felt like it or happened to wake up early in the morning? And what if you told him that you would participate in swim meets only when you had nothing better to do that day?"

Matt: "You've got to be kidding. If I said this, I'd get kicked off the team."

Fr. Tom: "You mean your coach is that narrow-minded? Isn't it unreasonable to expect someone to devote all that time to practice and then give half a day away on the weekends to attend swim meets?"

Matt: "If we weren't in top-notch shape and used to daily practice, we would lose to our opponents, and no one wants that to happen. In this city swimming is a big thing. Competition is stiff. If we don't take extraordinary measures in practice, we don't stand a chance of winning."

Fr. Tom: "No doubt you went to practice whether you felt like it or not, right? Now let's talk about God's team. What if he said that the team would practice only one day a week for an hour, and if you didn't really feel like going you didn't have to? And...that no one would get kicked off the team? How many games do you think God's team would win?"

Matt: "None of course. If a coach is too easy on his players, the team will fall apart and end up getting their, you-know-what's, kicked every week. Are you telling me that God has a team? Are you telling me that I'm on it?"

Fr. Tom: "We've already talked about evil in the world and souls going through the wide gate to destruction. Do you think God can just sit back and watch those he created in his own image, be destroyed? Why do you think he sent Jesus? Why did Jesus form a team of disciples to share his work? He came on earth to engage the enemy and to get back from Satan those people whom he stole from God. When a person is baptized, they are enlisted as part of God's "team." As they grow up, they decide whether or not to accept the challenge to work with God. If a person says, "Yes, I want God's team to win, but I'm not willing to go to practice for even one hour a week, and be part of his work," what would you think?

Matt: "I guess God would kick that person off the team and stick with those who were willing to put in practice time. That's what a good coach would do."

Fr. Tom: "So the minimum expectations are that you put in one hour each Sunday as a member of God's team. Even that is not enough. Anyone who would skip a one-hour, one-day-a-week practice, has no right to be on God's team or receive the rewards this brings."

Matt: "I guess if God were a pushover coach, the Christians would never come out on top, would they? And I guess my whining about Sunday Mass must stop. I'm glad that I put in extra, voluntary "practice" on Friday evenings."

Fr. Tom: "How many hours per day do your think the devil works trying to steal souls away from God? Just an hour or so a week? I don't think so. The devil means business and most of God's people don't. Are we surprised that when we look at our world, the devil seems to be winning hands down?"

Matt: "This is heavy duty stuff, Fr. Tom. Does God really mean business, the way our swim coach does?"

Fr. Tom: "Yes. If he didn't mean business, why did he send his only Son to earth to suffer and die? Doesn't that send a message about how important winning souls is to him? When he sees his children heading down the wrong road, imagine how it upsets him. Have you read yet about the requirements Jesus put on his followers? They had to leave everything to follow him. They had to put all of their time and energy at his disposal. He was a demanding coach, because he knew how great the stakes were in the game of life. He knew that human beings on their own could not stand up to the devil's team.

Fr. Tom: "The fact is, Matt, that not everyone who goes to Church—even those who go weekly—are disciples of Jesus. They may stand on the sidelines and cheer a little, but they are not out there playing the game. Jesus is looking for disciples who will be part of his team rather than church-goers who are half-hearted about following him."

Matt: "Do you think Jesus wants me to be a disciple, Fr. Tom? Honestly, from what you say, I don't think I've really joined Jesus' team yet. I am not what you would call a disciple, any more than a guy who takes a leisurely swim now and then is part of the swim team. How can I become a disciple of Jesus? Do you think he is calling me to go all out for him, the way I go all out for swimming?"

Fr. Tom: "You are asking the most important question any human can answer. There are stories in the Bible of men who asked Jesus the same question. It would be interesting to read the stories and see how Jesus responded. Some turned down Jesus' invitation to follow him. This is such an important question that it would be worth your while to talk to Jesus about it on Friday night."

Chapter 6

Matt: "One of the religion teachers said that rules and regulations are not that important as long as we love other people. And yet the Bible is filled with rules isn't it? For example, is there anything wrong with copying homework or cheating on the ACT exam? I'm sure you can't find anything about homework or ACT in the Bible. Cheating doesn't really hurt anyone, and it can boost the grade of the one who does it. This confuses me."

Fr. Tom: "You drive a car, don't you Matt? What do you put in the gas tank? How much does it cost you?"

Matt: "That's a silly question, Fr. Tom. Of course, I put in gasoline and it costs about three dollars a gallon...maybe forty dollars for a fill up."

Fr. Tom: "You want to save money, don't you Matt? I'll give you an idea for cutting your gasoline costs in half. For every gallon of gasoline, you put in, follow this with a gallon of water. This will reduce your costs by 50%. With this strategy you can fill the tank for about twenty dollars."

Matt: "This might save money, but it will destroy the car by mixing water with gasoline."

Fr. Tom: "Says who?"

Matt: "Everyone knows that cars burn gasoline to create energy, and water doesn't burn."

Fr. Tom: "Are you sure. Have you ever tried it?"

Matt: "Of course I've never been dumb enough to put water in the gas tanks. The car manufacturers build cars to operate on gasoline. So that's why everyone puts gasoline in their tanks. The guys who made the car know what works and what doesn't."

Fr. Tom: "How dare the car manufacturers tell you what you can do and cannot do with your own car? Who are they to put restrictions on your freedom? Don't you have the right to put water in your tank if you want to?"

Matt: "Sure, I guess I have the right. But, then I'll have a car that won't take me any place."

Fr. Tom: "Now back to rules. The manufacturer makes a car according to a certain plan. Among other things, it burns gasoline to create the power needed to push the car along the road. We can break the rules if we want, but then our cars won't work. So, we respect what the operating manuals say about the cars we buy. They are not trying to oppress us with silly rules; they want us to enjoy riding in the car with as few problems as possible. If we go against the advice of the manufacturers, we end up with a car that doesn't work. So, what am I trying to say?"

Matt: "I guess that God is the "manufacturer" who put us together. He knows what works and what doesn't. He knows what will make us happier and what will steal happiness. It is not like he's putting arbitrary rules on us; it's that he knows what works and what doesn't. He is smarter than we are, just as the car manufacturer is smarter about the cars they produce than we are. That makes sense."

Fr. Tom: "So how does this apply to cheating in school?"

Matt: "The Bible doesn't say anything about this, so how do we know if this helps us be happier or makes us feel worse. Conscience?"

Fr. Tom: "Yes, our consciences are built in truth detectors put there by the "manufacturer." Sometimes our consciences are confused because of lies that other people might tell us, so we have the Bible to let us know what's right and what's wrong."

Matt: "But suppose someone thinks it's okay to cheat on a test, and their conscience doesn't bother them. And, even if they look in the Bible, there's nothing there about cheating on tests, is there?"

Fr. Tom: "If we have a poorly formed conscience, then we learn what's good for us and bad for us the hard way. After a while we begin to experience the negative results of breaking God's rules. As a matter of fact, the Bible does talk about cheating on tests. It's called the "8th commandment." This commandment reminds us not to lie. Jesus also spoke against lying. When we cheat, we are telling ourselves and others that we are better than we really are - that's a lie. And I think both of us know from experience the uneasy feeling we have inside when we get a grade we don't deserve. We are less happy. The "manufacturer" knows what works for us and what doesn't. He wants us to be as happy as we possibly can. Telling the truth is always the best way to go, even if it means getting a low grade on the ACT.

In case you don't know, there is a book called the, "Catechism of the Catholic Church," that develops and explains what's in the Bible. With the "8th commandment," for example, there are about "50" different items in the Catechism helping us to understand what a lie is and what it isn't. You might want to look this up. It is the official supplement to the "owner's manual."

"Another way to look at this is in terms of swim meets. Why can't someone dive into the water a second before the gun goes off? Why can't people wear swim fins in a race? Why can't people switch lanes and bump into one of the other competitors? Think of what would happen if people made up their own rules in a swim meet? It would be chaos, right?

We live in a society today that ignores God's rules and makes up their own. Isn't this what the devil encouraged Adam and Eve to do? When we make up our own rules, chaos follows, and our "cars" quit running. Human beings have begun to pretend that they are gods, that they own their own bodies, and that they can do anything they want, and things will work out well.

Guess I've made my point. Wise people have always sought out God's way so they can live a happier, more prosperous life. This wisdom is available to us if we seek it out."

Chapter 7

Matt: "My friends don't see a point in going to confession. One of the kids goes to a non-Catholic Christian church, and they don't believe in confessing your sins to a priest. After all, why can't they confess them straight to God? What's the purpose of a "middleman?" Besides when you read about all the priests who have been involved in sexual abuse, can you really trust telling your sins to a priest? I don't know anyone who goes to confession."

Fr. Tom: "Remember the talk we had about car manufacturers who know what's best for the smooth running of their cars? If confession is part of God's plan for the smooth running of our lives, then maybe we have to take his word for it. It is okay to confess your sins directly to God, of course. Why then did God set up a system in which we are encouraged to confess our sins to a priest? Do you see any advantages to this, Matt?

Matt: "Well it feels good to get something off your chest—to tell a trusted friend or one of your parents. I guess telling it to God leaves doubt about whether we really are sorry and whether or not

God really forgives us. A guy in our class is in a twelve-step program and he confesses his sins to a sponsor."

Fr. Tom: "Jesus came to us as a human being, someone we could see and relate to. Most of the time he touched people and spoke to people rather than helping them from a distance. It means more to us when we can have personal contact with a human being, than just imagining we are in contact with God. That is why Jesus set up the sacraments. He continues being present on earth in a concrete way each time the Church celebrates the sacraments. When a priest, for example, baptizes someone, he pours real water, says real words, touches the person, and in doing this he represents the real Jesus to them. This is not a make-believe ceremony in which a person imagines himself or herself being saved. When we sin, guilt hangs on us, and we want the assurance we are forgiven by God. Jesus made it clear to his apostles that, "whose sins you shall forgive they are forgiven." He gave these special humans the same power he had as God's Son to forgive sins. The ordained priests stand in the position of the apostles. When the priest says, "I absolve you from all your sins," we know with certainty that Jesus himself has spoken to us. There is a sense of freedom that we don't get by limiting our confession to God alone. Through the Sacrament of Reconciliation, Jesus adds an extra layer of grace and forgiveness."

Matt: "That makes sense. But what if the priest is one of the pedophiles, does it still count?"

Fr. Tom: "I think most of the priests who were involved in such crimes are out of ministry now. On the other hand, if an expert plumber fixes the leaky pipes in your home and it turns out he is a pedophile, are the pipes still fixed?"

Matt: "Yes, his moral life has nothing to do with his work as a plumber. So, a priest is doing God's work in hearing confessions, and the state of his own soul doesn't really come into it."

Fr. Tom: "Let me also remind you that a priest must keep the seal of confession, even if it costs him his life. He is not permitted to tell anything he's heard in confession, under the pain of serious sin. I've never heard of a priest leaking out information he heard in the confessional, but if he did, he must go to the bishop himself to receive forgiveness for this sin. The sanctity of the confessional surpasses all codes of confidentiality that exists in our society."

Fr. Tom: "I will also note that people can be picky in choosing a confessor. There have been times in which a certain priest did not do a good job in representing the compassion of Jesus. Ask God to lead you to a helpful confessor.

One more note is that there is a special grace in the Sacrament of Reconciliation that gives strength to resist sinning again. This is not available to those who limit confession of sins to private prayer or even to a 12-step sponsor."

Matt: "Okay. I must admit that I haven't been to confession since 8th grade. I'm afraid to go. What will the priest think of me?"

Fr. Tom: "The priest will admire your courage and gladly give you the forgiveness of Jesus."

Fr. Tom: "Back to one of our first conversations. I challenged you to visit Jesus in Eucharistic adoration to test it out—to find out if he is real. You tried it and it worked. The same thing about confession. We could discuss all day the pros and cons of this sacrament, but talking about the experience doesn't replace the actual reception of the sacrament. Try it and see. Then let me know if it made a difference in your life. Did it add anything to asking forgiveness from God without using a "middleman?" Then when you talk to your friends about going to confession, you can add the results of your personal experience to the conversation."

Matt: "But I forgot the procedure I am supposed to use. How can I get around that?"

Fr. Tom: "Many people have forgotten the procedure. No big deal. Just begin by telling the priest that you've forgotten and need him to coach you through the process. Priests are used to doing this. This is not a rigid process; it is meant to be a relaxed, healing encounter with Jesus Christ himself. You've read enough of the Gospels to know how people's lives were changed when they met Jesus. Those people have nothing on us. In the Sacrament of Reconciliation, we can have the same kind of experience with Jesus as they did. Amazing the Catholic Church! And do you know that all priests are sinners too. We probably go to confession more than anyone does.

Chapter 8

Matt: "A Christian friend of mine told me that Jesus is not really present in the bread and wine at Mass. He told me that his pastor said that this is only a symbol of Jesus, not really his body and blood. The pastor quoted the Bible where Jesus said, "Do this in remembrance of me." That means we are just recalling something in the past to help us remember Jesus. I didn't know how to answer this. How can I prove that the bread and wine at Mass are truly the body and blood of the real Jesus?"

Fr. Tom: "Do you know that the polls tell us the majority of Catholics do not believe in the real presence of Jesus in the Eucharist, even though the Church clearly teaches that it is, and the Bible does the same. This is a crisis in the Church now, and the point that your friend made seems to represent the thinking of most Catholics. The bishops of the United States are so concerned about this that they are producing a special document to help Catholics refocus on what we really believe about the Eucharist."

Fr. Tom: "I suggest you read the sixth chapter of the Gospel of John. Jesus says that he is the "bread of life." And bread is something we eat. He didn't say he was like a piece of bread. In the same passage he says that "Whoever eats my flesh and drinks my blood has life in him," and goes on to say, "Unless you eat my flesh and drink my blood you will not have life in you." He is so clear about this and so repetitive that it upset those who listened to him. In fact, St. John reports that many of his disciples left him because of this. They would not have left him if they thought he was talking symbolically, would they?

Besides this, for 2000 years in the Church it has been the clear belief that Jesus meant what he said. Thousands of books have been written on this, and many Christians were martyred because they would not retract their belief in the real presence of Jesus in the Eucharist. If you go to the Catechism of the Catholic Church, you will find great explanations of this. There may be Protestant services where bread is blessed and handed out as a symbol of the Last Supper. At Mass, however, the bread and wine are changed, by the prayer of the priest, into the living Body and Blood of Jesus."

Matt: "I accept this Fr. Tom, but how can you prove it?"

Fr Tom: "For me, I was brought up as a Catholic and accepted this truth without questioning it. Later in life, prior to becoming a priest, I began to doubt this, especially when I met with people who laughed off the idea. One day as I was trying to figure this out, the thought came to me that, if God is a loving Father, would he let generations upon generations of Christians be deceived into thinking this is really Jesus if it wasn't? And, in my life, would he teach me over and over this truth, and, in fact be tricking me into a lie? Of course not. God in his love speaks only the truth to us. Then, like a light bulb going on inside my head, the issue was resolved. God means what he says. And what a wonderful gift that he would give us Jesus in as physical a way as this. There are no bounds to God's love.

Also, we watch miracles take place each day that we can't explain. Take a tiny tomato seed for example. How can this little thing get buried into the ground and then produce a hundred tomatoes? Has any scientist ever invented a tomato seed? Scientists can manipulate life, but they can't produce even one tomato unless they take the seed and the dirt that God gave them to work with. And when we acknowledge that God's only Son came from heaven and became a human being by a miraculous move of the Holy Spirit within the womb of Mary, we are awestruck. Is there anything impossible to our God? Our Protestant friends believe that Jesus is both God and man, don't they? If God can share his Son under the appearances of a human being, then why can't he continue to do so under the simple appearances of bread and wine?

Matt: "So this is just a matter of faith, with no proof involved?"

Fr Tom: "I suggest you ask God to reveal to you this truth in a personal way, as he did with me, so it goes from a Church belief to a personal belief."

Also, I suggest you do as you did with adoration. Next time you receive communion, ask Jesus to reveal himself to you in a special way, as he is brought from the altar into your body. Talk to him as though he were really there. See what happens.

Finally think of a problem in your life that you can't resolve. Maybe a sin that you keep committing or a relationship that isn't working out or a worry that keeps plaguing you. Start receiving communion as though it is a "medicine" that will heal you from this issue. See what happens over a period of time and see if this issue begins to resolve because of the unique presence of Jesus that comes into you at Mass. Start gathering personal "evidence" to prove that Jesus is truly present in bodily form in the Eucharist."

Matt: "You've got me thinking, Fr. Tom. When you talk about Jesus as a real person, it makes more sense than the empty talk that went on in my religion classes. I'm beginning to see that he is really the answer to my deepest questions, and that without him, nothing in my life makes much sense. I'll see you next week with more questions.

Chapter 9

Matt: "Well Parker and I had a long talk this weekend. He still doesn't buy into much of what you've been telling me. He conceded that heaven may exist, but his life here and now is all that counts. He wants to have fun while he's on this earth. Then he threw this at me: suppose I buy into the heaven idea and try to follow Jesus throughout my life. And then, when I die suppose this has all been a trick, and I found out that heaven, as the atheists claim, was just a religious hoax. Then what?"

Fr. Tom: "Okay, Matt. Suppose you have 20 dollars and head out to the racetrack. In the first race there are only two horses running: "Heaven" and "No Heaven." You can bet on one or the other. If you bet on "Heaven" and it wins the race, you get a paid vacation to an island paradise—worth about ten thousand dollars. On the other hand, if "No Heaven" wins, and you bet on "Heaven," you lose twenty bucks. And if "No Heaven" wins, the reward you win is just ten dollars. Which horse would you bet on?"

Matt: "Heaven" of course. If I lose, I'm only out twenty dollars. If I bet on "No Heaven," the best I can do is get my twenty bucks back and add ten more dollars."

Fr. Tom: "Do you get my point? If you spend your life betting on "Heaven" and your right, you win an eternity of ecstatic happiness. If you bet on "No Heaven" and you win—that is when you die, that's it, there's nothing—then all you gained was a few years of fun on this earth. In the first case you win everything; in the second case, even if you're right, you win practically nothing.

Apart from that, however. If someone takes Jesus Christ seriously and allows him into their hearts, they have a piece of heaven even before they die. Those who have done this testify that the happiness that Jesus brings is much greater than all the "fun times" they had without him. You might read about St. Augustine and his personal experience with Jesus. So even if "No Heaven" wins, being with Jesus in this life is the best way to go."

Matt: "I can testify to that. Since I started taking Jesus seriously, my life has been more peaceful, I get along better with my parents, and that rejection I used to feel has disappeared."

Fr. Tom: "Let me give you another angle on this. You are finishing up high school now. Suppose the state made a new rule that you must continue for another year or two in high school, how would you like that?"

Matt: "I wouldn't. I've had enough high school; I want to graduate and move on to another phase of my life."

Fr. Tom: "Now suppose someone says that all there is to life is high school, and you must stay there till you die?"

Matt: "I couldn't think of a worse scenario. Four years of high school is more than enough. I want to get out into the real world and be freed from the restrictions of high school. As you know, my hope is to get a college degree if I can work it out."

Fr. Tom: "High school is like a four-year journey to a new land. We don't want to be there forever. And if all there is to life is perpetual high school, we'd get pretty depressed, wouldn't we?"

Fr. Tom: "There is a popular view of life called 'secularism' that says life on earth is all there is. We don't ever graduate to heaven. And so our goal is to make the most of it while we're here. The Christian "world view" says that life on earth is a short journey to our real homeland. Looking at life from this point of view, we consider life now as being "in exile." We can't be perfectly happy here, because we are on a trip to our homeland. And so, we keep taking steps forward to help us arrive there safely.

With the worldview of secularism, there is no real goal. We don't realize we're in exile and so we don't know where we're headed. We may even find ourselves walking around in circles with no purpose in life. It is like staying in high school indefinitely.

Christians buy into a "Biblical worldview." We believe in the story that the Bible tells that there is a God who wants to be our Father, and he wants us to be home with him. He sent Jesus as the "tour guide" who alone knows how to get us where God wants us to go. Follow him and we make it home. Try a different way and we end up in the land of perpetual misery, which we call "hell."

It is really important to examine both worldviews, because on most college campuses, as I understand, the professors are pushing the secular worldview, and most college kids are buying into it. Getting the truth into your head now will protect you from following self-appointed "tour guides" who lead us down the road to destruction. The more you read the Bible and listen to Jesus, the more you will realize that life on this planet is a journey, not our final home.

God sent Jesus to us as the sure way to make it to our homeland. If you went to a strange city and wanted to visit a tourist sight, you can either start driving around randomly, following your own thoughts and hoping to accidentally get where you want to go, or you can ask someone who's lived in that city all their life to show you how to reach this destination. Would you try it your way or put your trust in the resident who knows the city like the back of his hand? You could waste time, money, and peace of mind by following your own lead and never get to where you want to go, or you could ask the resident to take you there.

What's the point? Jesus is already in the homeland, and he also lived on this earth. He knows exactly how to get you where you want to go, and the shortest route to get there. Doesn't it make sense to follow him, rather than try our "random" approach or listen to people who don't even believe there is the tourist attraction in the first place?"

Matt: "I think somewhere in the Bible Jesus said that he is "the way." That makes more sense in the context of our need for tour guides in a strange city."

Fr. Tom: "You're on target again Matt. In fact, Jesus said He is "the way, the truth, and the life." That means that He not only is the way home, all other ways are fake. Jesus is the only truth. And along the way, the "life" Jesus offers even during our "earth tour" is a hundred times more satisfying than what the "fake guides" offer us. Jesus offers us inner happiness now and the inner assurance that we are investing well our lives on this planet."

Matt: "Thanks, Fr. Tom, for giving me so much of your time. I wish religion class would have been this helpful. I want to meet with you one more time. The only other question I have right now is about prayer. Oh, I forgot to tell you that Parker went to adoration with me last Friday, and he said it wasn't as bad as he thought it would be. Progress, huh?"

Chapter 10

Matt: "Final question. How do you pray? Is it real or just something that goes on in your imagination? I get adoration, I get Mass, and I'm starting to get more out of confession, but when I pray, I don't get much out of it."

Fr. Tom: "Tell me about your experience with prayer."

Matt: "Well, I ask God for things, like help on a test, or that my dad would get off my case, or that I make a good decision about college. And then sometimes I say the prayers I learned in grade school like the Our Father and the Hail Mary. My mom wants me to say the rosary but that's too boring for me. Then before I go to bed, I usually say 'Goodnight God, thanks for this day.'"

Fr. Tom: "Nothing against asking God for things or reciting rote prayers, but I like the "Goodnight God" prayer the best. This is a moment in which you are addressing God in a more personal way. When we limit our prayers to asking God for help, we are not building a relationship with him. For example, if the only communication you have with your parents is asking them for money, the car, or other things, not much of a relationship is being established. You are treating them like some kind of snack machine where you punch a button, and it gives you what you need. As you get older, you will find it helpful to establish a different kind of relationship with your parents, in which you talk things over with them or listen to their thoughts or even share your feelings with them.

Relationships are more important than the "snack machine" approach. Same with God. You are getting to enjoy being alone with Jesus; let prayer focus on the relationship. Be honest in telling Jesus how you feel. Ask him questions that bother you. Listen to what he speaks in your heart about how he feels toward you and what he thinks of you.

Nothing wrong with asking favors, but the biggest favor is having a rewarding friendship with Jesus. Though he is the Son of God, he also offers his friendship to you. Some people find it helpful to write him letters—like a journal—and try to sense how he is receiving what you say. When we focus on the relationship, the things that we need seem to get taken care of.

There is a verse in Matthew's gospel, where Jesus says, "Seek first the Kingdom of God, and all the other things will be given you besides." We might paraphrase this by saying, "Seek first to grow closer to Jesus and follow him, and everything else will fall into place."

Matt: "So just talking to Jesus as a friend and trying to learn from him is prayer?"

Fr. Tom: "In my opinion it is the best of prayers."

Matt: "What about the rosary and rote prayers I was forced to memorize when I was in grade school. Are these worth saying?"

Fr Tom: "What's your opinion, Matt?"

Matt: "I guess if I think about what I'm saying and say them as though I'm really talking to a person instead of just doing a recitation, they probably have their value."

Fr. Tom: "You took the words out of my mouth. Remember that the "Our Father" is addressed to Jesus' Father, whom we call God. He is a dad, the perfect dad, just as Jesus is the perfect friend. Each phrase of the 'Our Father' has a deep meaning. If you read the Catechism of the Catholic Church, there are many pages devoted to explaining the meaning of each part of this prayer. When, for example, we say 'Thy Kingdom come,' we are asking that each of us develops a close, fulfilling relationship with God as our Father—the kind that

Adam and Eve once had in the garden, before they cut themselves off from God. When we say, "Lead us not into temptation," we are asking him to keep us on the right track and not let us get pulled away from him the way our first parents did. It is better to recite one Our Father slowly than to say a bunch of them without thinking what we're saying."

Matt: "That makes sense. What about the 'Hail Mary."

Fr. Tom: "From what you say, you have a wonderful mother, Matt. Chances are, however, she has her faults and failings. When Jesus hung on the cross, he gave every one of his disciples his mother as their mother too. Christians, then, are entitled to a relationship with Jesus' own mother as being their mother. She is the perfect mother. So, when we say the 'Hail Mary' we are coming before our new mother and developing a relationship with her. Say it slowly and reflect on each phrase. You will find out that the whole first part of the prayer consists of Bible quotes that were addressed to her. Once again, the Catechism, has lots to say about Mary and the meaning of this prayer.

Matt: "What about the fact that many prayers people say are not answered? Why does God hold back favors from people? And why does he allow evil in the world?"

Fr. Tom: "Pretend you are a kind and wealthy dad, and your son asked you for something, would you give it to him?"

Matt: "I guess so, as long as it wouldn't bring him harm. If he asked for a lot of money, I might say no because he may use it irresponsibly. Generally, though, I think I would give him what he asks for."

Fr. Tom: "Isn't God the same way. He wants to do good things for his children. He wants us to ask so He can show us how much he loves us. And sure, maybe some things we aren't ready for yet, and he will give them to us at a future date. For example, if we ask him to take us to heaven, he probably won't grant it immediately. He will wait until the time ordained for us to die. And maybe the prayer he most wants to answer us is that we learn to get closer to him, rather than that he gives us stuff or makes our lives more comfortable. You know from sports, that discipline is needed to be a good athlete more than an easy life might be. God wants us to be strong and self-controlled, not spoiled brats."

"And, why God allows evil in the world? There are libraries written on this. You might want to think it out yourself. Remember our story of Adam and Eve. All evil goes back to being separated from God—not having a close relationship with him. Once Adam and Eve decided to pull away from God other evils followed. It's like putting lemonade in your gas tank. Once you start doing this, the car begins to break down. The evil in the world all stems from people not having a right relationship with God. If God magically erased all evil from the world tomorrow and people were still out of relationship with him, guess what? Evil would start being generated all over again, because evil begins inside the human heart and spreads from there. When two kids get in a fight, for example, it's because of some kind of anger and hatred in their hearts. It wouldn't do any good for God to step in and stop all fights, because that doesn't eliminate what's inside people's hearts or bring people closer to him."

"If God, for example, stopped all wars tomorrow and there was "peace on earth," would we really be better off? If peace frees us to go on being selfish and live as though God doesn't exist, it is fake peace. There would still be no peace inside the hearts of people."

Matt: "So I guess it all goes back to Jesus, huh? Until a person lets Jesus in their lives, they will be broken on the inside and separated from God. They won't be happy and will probably go around making the world worse off than it already is. When people turn to Jesus and link up with him, then peace starts coming into their hearts and it will start spreading to those around them. If enough people get connected with Jesus, there won't be enough hate in the world to start another war."

"Let me tell you that our sessions have changed my life. My parents are the first ones to notice that there's been a change in me. My friends too. Others are starting to ask me the same kinds of questions I've been asking you. This "Jesus stuff" is pretty contagious, isn't it?

Thank you for your time, and you can bet that I will be knocking on your door when I face new issues in my life."

Fr. Tom: "These conversations have helped me as much as they've helped you. I'm glad to talk with you Matt any time you want.

I want to share one more thought with you. It was given me when I was a senior in high school by Brother Robert. It goes back to our talk about worldview. We had a blackboard that stretched all the way across the front of the classroom. Brother Robert took a piece of chalk and, starting at the far-left side of the board, drew a line all the way to the end of the right side. Then he stepped back and said to us, "This is your life." Next, he walked down to the far left side again, and about an inch from the end, he drew a hatch mark. Pointing to the one-inch segment, he said, "And this is your life on earth." He went on to say that the "one inch" part of our lives was all about making a decision where we wanted to spend the rest of it. Each day we make small decisions to draw closer to God or to move further away from him. Eventually all these little decisions mound up to one big decision. Have we decided to follow Jesus and make him the most important person in our lives or not?

You have come to an important turning point in your life, Matt. You have begun to follow Jesus. You have begun to build a strong decision that will carry you into heaven. Every day you have opportunities to strengthen this decision. Eventually, following Jesus, will become a lifestyle for you, and you will be helping to insure where you will spend the greatest part of your life.

And, oh yes. When you talk to Jesus, please ask him to help me be a better priest."

www.ingramcontent.com/pod-product-compliance
Lightning Source LLC
Chambersburg PA
CBHW021937170626
46807CB00007B/3161